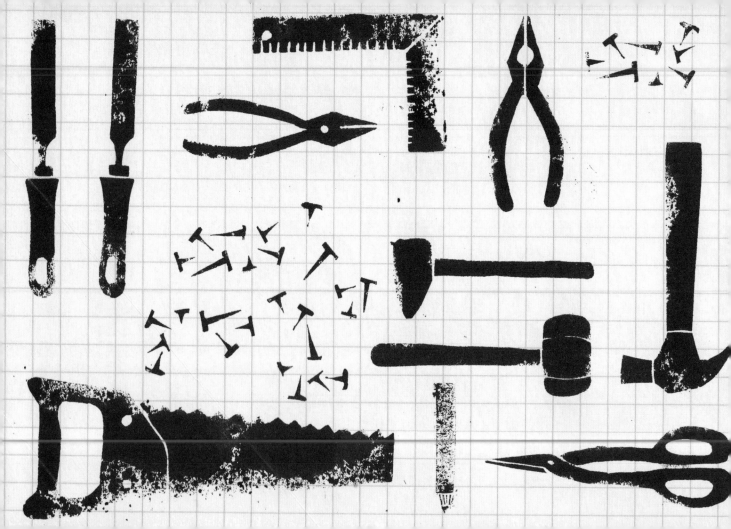

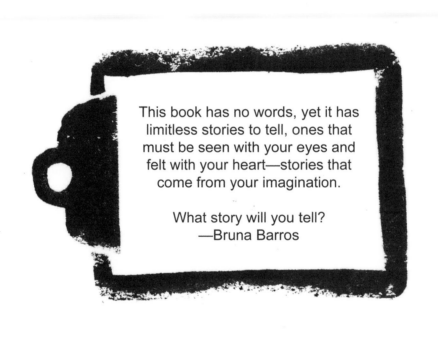

This book has no words, yet it has limitless stories to tell, ones that must be seen with your eyes and felt with your heart—stories that come from your imagination.

What story will you tell?
—Bruna Barros

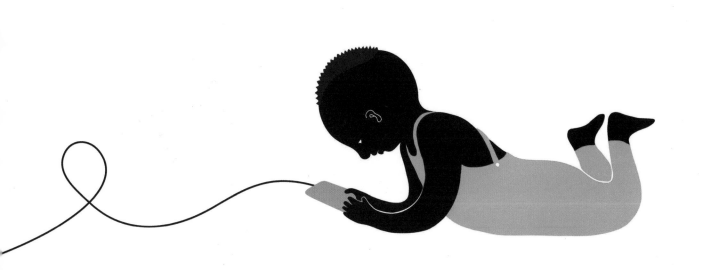

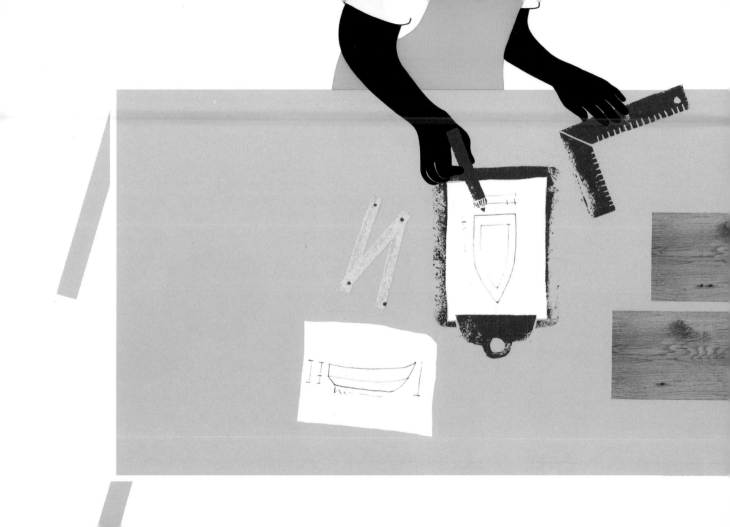

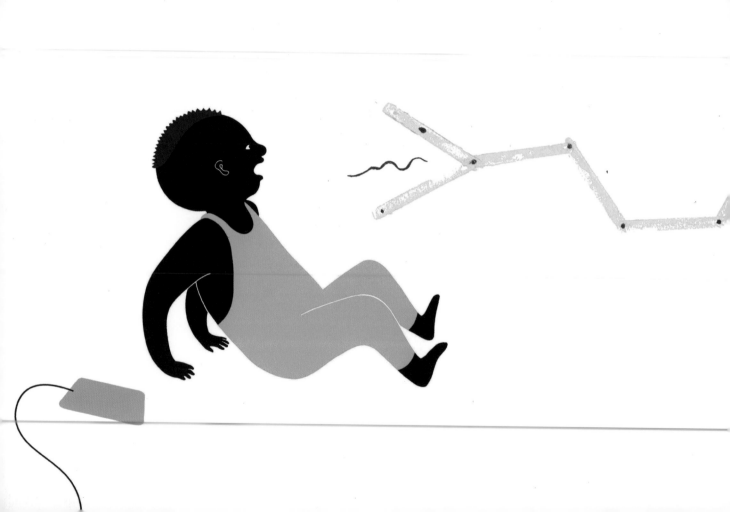

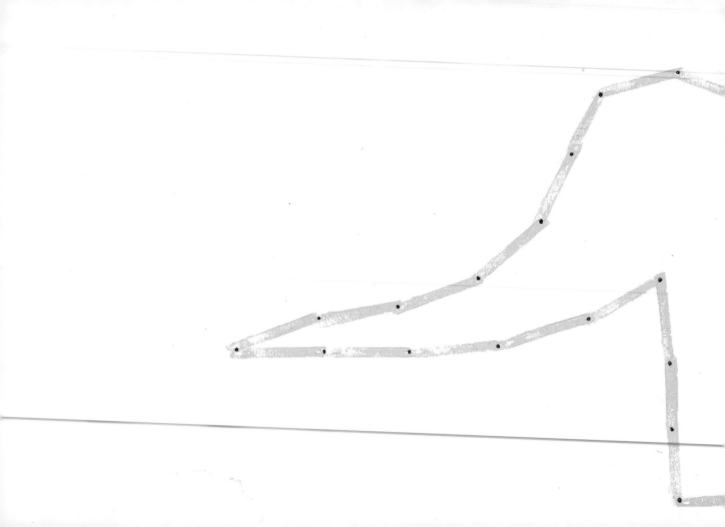

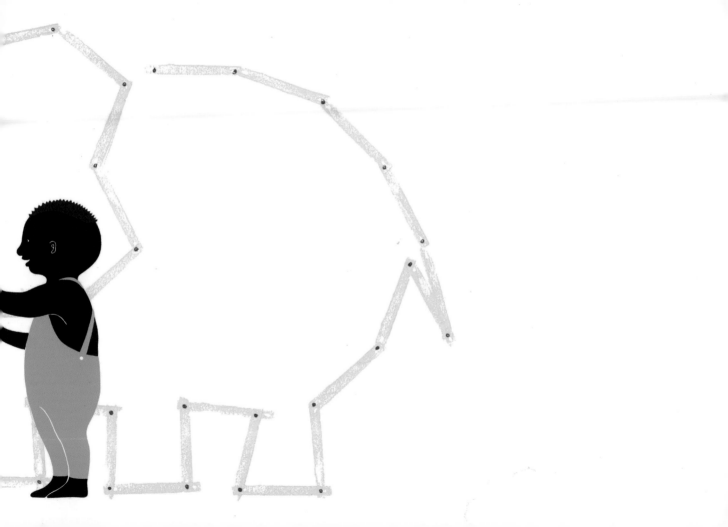

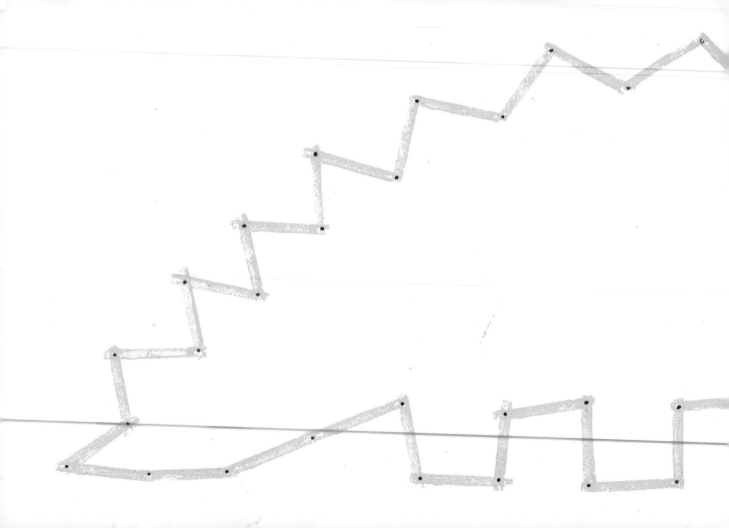

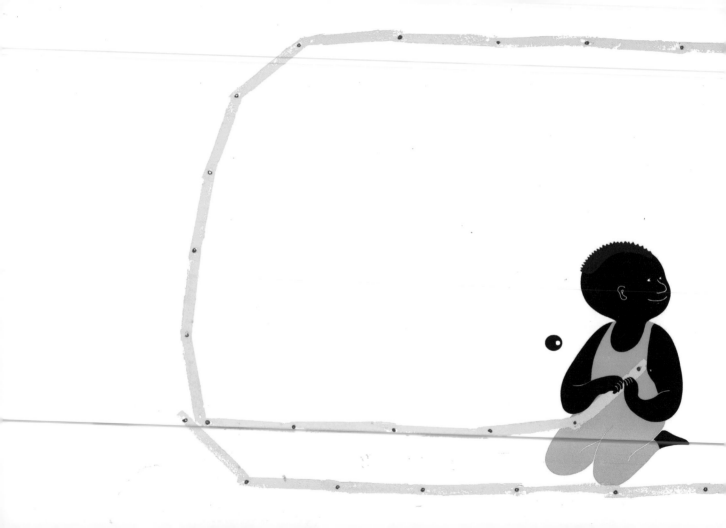

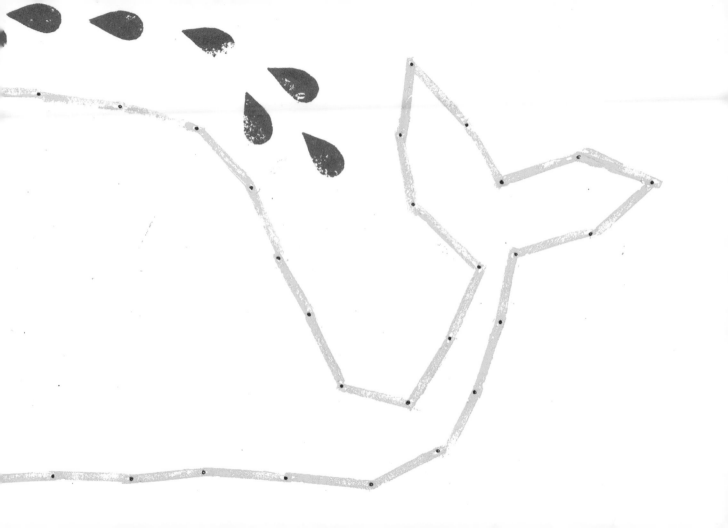

Manufactured in Hong Kong in October 2016 by Toppan Printing, Co.

Published in Brazil by LEMOS Editorial
Title of the original edition: *O carpinteiro*
© 2015 by LEMOS Editorial, Brazil
© 2015 text and illustrations by Bruna Barros

Published in the United States by Gibbs Smith
21 20 19 18 17   5 4 3 2 1

Gibbs Smith
P.O. Box 667
Layton, Utah 84041

1.800.835.4993 orders
www.gibbs-smith.com

Designed by Bruna Barros
Gibbs Smith books are printed on either recycled, 100% post-consumer
waste, FSC-certified papers or on paper produced from sustainable PEFC-
certified forest/controlled wood source. Learn more at www.pefc.org.

Library of Congress Control Number: 2016945725
ISBN: 978-1-4236-4676-1

After studying fashion design and interior design in Belo Horizonte, Brazil, Bruna Barros switched directions to focus on art. She spent two years at the Academy of Fine Arts of Venice, working closely with children, while she earned a degree in Graphic Arts. She has illustrated eight children's books.

brunabarrosillustration.com

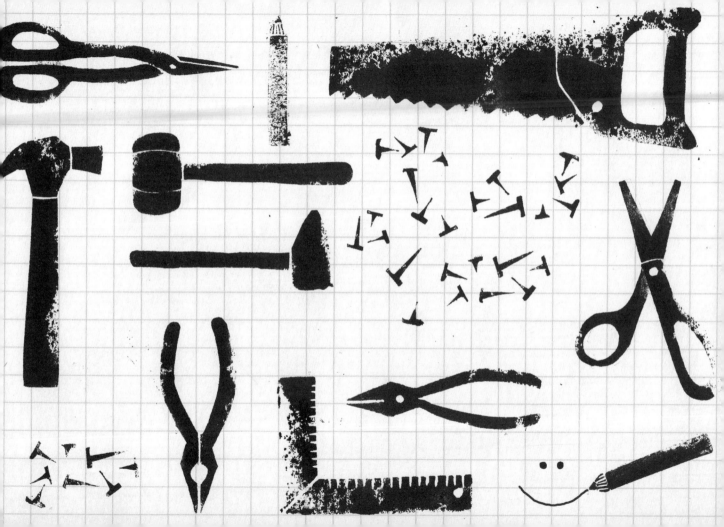

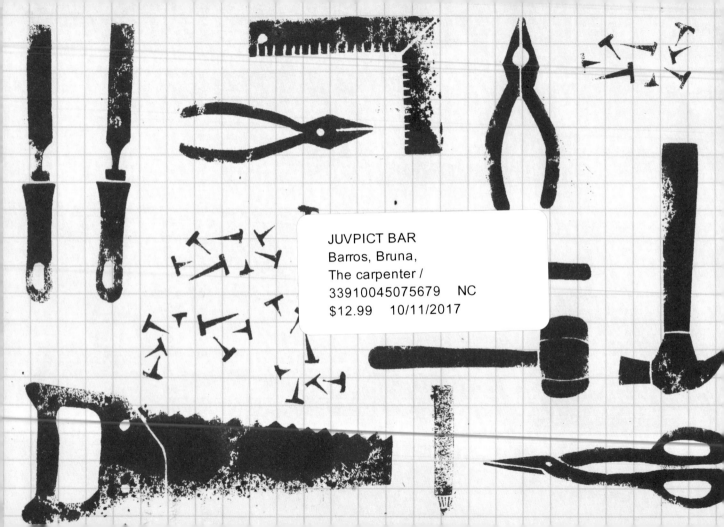